Getting Ready for My First Day of School

Getting Ready for My First Day of School

William L. Coleman

BETHANY HOUSE PUBLISHERS
MINNEAPOLIS, MINNESOTA 55438
A Division of Bethany Fellowship, Inc.

Photos by Dick Easterday and Larry Swenson.

Verses marked TLB are taken from The Living Bible, copyright © 1971 by Tyndale House Publishers, Wheaton, Ill. Used by permission.

Published by Bethany House Publishers
A Division of Bethany Fellowship, Inc.
6820 Auto Club Road, Minneapolis, MN 55438

Printed in the United States of America

Library of Congress Cataloging in Publication Data

Coleman, William L.
    Getting ready for my first day of school.
    Summary: A series of fifty-one readings dealing with the activities which are part of the school experience, some with a religious emphasis, and useful in preparing a child going to school for the first time.
    1. Children—Prayer-books and devotions—English.
[1. Schools.   2. Christian life]   I. Title.
BV4870.C6314   1983   242'.62   83-3809
ISBN 0-87123-274-X (pbk.)

A special thanks to Mary Coleman for typing the manuscript for this book.

About the Author

WILLIAM L. COLEMAN is very well known for his devotional books for young people. He is a graduate of Washington Bible College and Grace Theological Seminary. He has pastored three churches in three different states. He is a Staley Foundation lecturer and has written over 75 magazine articles. His by-line has appeared in *Christianity Today, Eternity, Campus Life,* and several other Christian magazines. He is married, the father of three children, and currently makes his home in Nebraska.

Note to Parents

The first day of school can be a traumatic experience not only for a child but also parents, especially if it's your first child starting or possibly the last to leave the nest. Now your beginner will have outside influence sometimes in disagreement with home philosophies. May I suggest that you don't just prepare your *child* for surprises but also educate yourself in the ways of school. Keep communication lines open between the teacher and yourself. School is the first important step in your child's lifetime journey. Make that first step a positive and meaningful one.

M. Maxine Lewin
Kindergarten teacher,
20 years

Helping Your Child

You are a thoughtful parent to take time to get your child ready for school. Your great attitude will serve your child well.

Consider a few ways you might use this book. How it works in your home will depend on your family and situation.

- One reading a day beginning in August will allow you to continue reading in September as your child adjusts to school.

- Three readings a week beginning in July will take 17 weeks and run into the school year.

- Some parents will want to read all of the book before school starts and then repeat chapters as the situations occur in school.

- Children differ greatly; your child may enjoy two readings a day in August and "reruns" in September.

Whichever method you decide fits your child best, remember the key words are patience, repetition, listening and a positive attitude. These are what make you such a good parent.

William L. Coleman
Aurora, Nebraska

Contents

Welcome to School

I am a teacher. I am glad you will be going to school soon. I will be there to welcome children to the class. I am a friend and helper.

School is an exciting place where you will meet new friends and do many special things.

You will go for nature walks, paint pictures, play with blocks and in the playhouse. There are many other fun toys to play with, too.

Fridays are special in my class because that is Show-and-Tell day. Children bring something from home to talk about and show their new friends.

I love children. I went to college to learn to teach children. I'm glad you are going to school. You are special!

Mrs. Donna Gerberling
Kindergarten teacher

People Are Different

It is exciting to meet
So many different people
In school.
Some will be tall or short,
Thin or big.

But each child will be
Someone special.

Some children will learn quickly.
And others will learn slowly.
A few will run very fast
And others will tag behind.

But each child will be
Someone special.

Maybe there will be children
In your classroom
Who have a different color skin
Than you have.
Some might be dark or light.
Their hair might be long, short,
Blonde, black, brown, or red.

But each child will be
Someone special.

Some children will get angry easily.
A few will talk loudly.

Some will talk so softly
You can barely hear them.

But each child will be
Someone special.

No two children will be the same.
No one will be exactly like you.
You won't be exactly like anyone else.

There are different children
Where you live
And where you go to church.
Now you will meet many more.

Do you ever wonder why God
Made us different?
Aren't you glad He did?
Now you can meet 10 or 20 new people.
It will be interesting
To know new people.

Each child will be
Someone special.

Jesus loved the little children.
That's why He held them closely.

"Then he took the children into his arms."
(Mark 10:16, TLB)

God Goes to School

Often we think about God
As if He lived
In some places,
But not in others.

It's easy to think
That God is in church.
We often believe God
Is in our house,
Or in our bedroom,
Because we talk
To Him there.

But actually, God doesn't live
In one place,
Or in two or three places.

God lives all around us
And He lives
Wherever we go.

God lives on the playground.
God lives on the bus.
God lives on the airplane.
God lives in the classroom.

When you get to school
God will be there—
Watching, listening, caring.

It feels good to know
That God goes to school, too!

"I will never leave thee." (Heb. 13:5, KJV)

Who Are You?

Two good things to know
When you go to school
Are your name and address.

Some children think they
Know where they live,
But they only know
Part of their address.

Maybe they know
What street they live on.
Maybe
They live on Eighth Street,
But they don't know
The house number.

Maybe another child knows
He lives at 718,
But doesn't know
What street he
Lives on.

It's important to know
All of your name
And all of your address.

If you forget
Part of your name or address,
Your teacher can help you
Remember.
But it's good
If you know both of them.

Learning to Build

Not everything in school
Will be new to you.
Your school will probably
Have building blocks,
And you have probably
Used building blocks before.

The blocks at school might be bigger,
And there might be more

Than you have ever used
Before.

Blocks are fun because
You can build houses,
And bridges and forts,
And fences and castles,
And garages and places
To hide.

In school it is
Extra fun
To build with blocks
Because you can do it
With other children.

You can learn new ideas
From them and
They can learn new ideas
From you.

When you build together
You share together,
You laugh together,
You learn together—
And you become friends.

Sometimes
You help your friends build
A large house
Just because they want it
That way.

Sometimes your friends
Will help you build

A wide house
Just because *you* want it
That way.

Building is important,
Especially when
You do it together.

Tell Your Family

When you get home
After your first day
At school,
You will have many things
To tell your family.

They will want to hear
About the games you played.
They will want to hear
About the stories you heard.
They will want to hear
About the songs you sang.

They will want to see
The papers you colored.
They will want to see
The things you made.
They will want to see
The letters you wrote.

They would like to know
What your room looks like.
They would like to know
Whom you sit beside.
They would like to know
What your walls look like
At school.

Your family wants to know
What your teacher is like.
What are your teacher's
Special things?

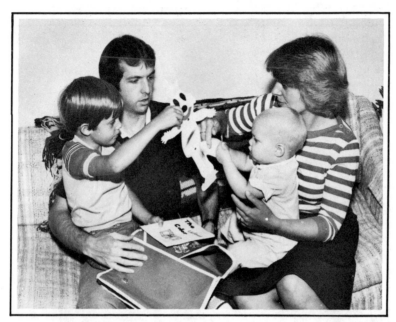

What does your teacher
Bring from home?
What do you like best
About your teacher?

Your family would like to know
What your teacher's name is.

They would also like to know
If there are special places
To play in your room.
Are there also special times
To play in your room?

You'll be busy
When you get home
From school.
There will be so much
To tell
Your family.

Stuffed Animals

Do you have any
Stuffed animals or dolls
That are special to you?

Do you have names
For them like Andy,
Susie, Freddy, Raggedy,
Snowball, Spot or Winnie?

Your stuffed animals
And dolls are special,
And you might miss them
While you are at school.

When you come home
From school,
You might want to
Play school
With your stuffed animals
And dolls.

You can line them up
On your bed
Or on the couch
Or in the backyard
And teach them
What you learned
In school today.

Stuffed animals and dolls
Are important to you.
And when you grow up,

You might still keep
A stuffed animal or two
On your bed.

Maybe
You would like to take
A stuffed animal
To school
Just for the day.

Ask your teacher
If it is okay.
If she says yes,
It will be fun
To take your
Stuffed animal
To school.

Away from Your Parents

Aren't parents great?
They are big and strong.
They love you,
Prepare good food for you,
Buy clothes for you,
And Dad can fix
Lots of things!

Many of us have two parents at home.
Some of us have only one.
But we can thank God
For the good parents we have.

Have you ever gone away
Without your parents?
Have you spent the night
At someone else's house,
Or had a baby-sitter;
Or have you gone to preschool?

Going to school will be
One of those times
When you will have to leave
Your parents.
That means
You are growing up
A little more.

We all leave our parents, sometime.
Your parents will be happy
When you go to school.

When you get home,
Tell your parents
All about your school.
They will be
Just as excited as you are.

Then give your parents
A big hug.
This will show them
That you think
They are really special people.

**"So give your parents joy!"
(Prov. 23:25, TLB)**

Dropping Things

Did you ever see a grown-up
Drop a glass or a plate?
Did you ever see a grown-up
Drop a ball or a book?

Everyone, of all ages,
Children, teenagers,
Grandparents, policemen,
Ball players, doctors,
Everyone drops things—
At one time or another.

Once in a while
People at school
Will drop something.

It might be a book.
It might be a block.
It might be a pail.
It might even be
A dish of paint!

We try not to drop things,
But we could have
An accident.

After we drop something,
We help pick it up,
Or we help clean it up,
Or we help put it back together.

Then we go back
To what we were doing.

What If?

Did you ever think,
What if I went to school,
And found out
They didn't have a bathroom?

What if I had to use
The bathroom,
And the school
Didn't have a bathroom?

It would be too far
To go home.
It would be hard
To go to a school
That didn't have
A bathroom!

That is why
There always is
A bathroom
In the school.

Schools also have
Water fountains,
Band-Aids,
Soap,
Telephones,
Paper towels,
And much more,
Just in case
You need them.

Your teacher knows about children.
Your teacher knows what you need.
And your teacher likes to help.

Putting on
Your Boots

You are getting bigger,
More grown-up than
You used to be.

Your parents are doing
Less for you
And you are doing
More for yourself.

Maybe you still need
Help with your coat,
But not as much help
As you used to need.

Zippers, snaps and buttons
Can be hard to work,
But you are doing them more easily
Because you practice
Zipping zippers,
Snapping snaps,
And buttoning buttons.

When you need help,
Your teacher can help,
But you won't need much
Because you are learning
To do it yourself.

Boots can be tricky.
Sometimes they are hard
To pull up over your shoe
Because your heel gets
In the way.

Sometimes they are hard
To buckle
Or snap
Or zip.

If you practice

At home,
You will get
Better at it.

Learning is fun,
Because you are
Growing up.

Are You Polite?

What does the word
Polite mean?
When you are kind
And wait for your turn
And don't interrupt
While others are talking,
You are polite.

You can be a good student
If you try to be polite.
This will become easy for you
Because you practice being polite at home.

You know when to say
"Thank you" and "please."
Sometimes you might forget,
But you often remember.

You also know how to ask permission.
At home you ask your parents
Before you cross the street,
Or go to a friend's house.

Otherwise your parents wouldn't find you
And they would worry.

You will want to be polite
At school, too.
You won't talk unless the teacher
Says it's your turn.
You won't get out of your seat
Until the teacher says you may.

If the teacher hands you something,
You should say "thank you."
If you need something,
You should say "please."

Everyone likes nice people.
Nice people know how
To be polite.

"Say 'Thank you' to the Lord for being so good, for always being so loving and kind." (Ps. 107:1, TLB)

Let's Pretend

Let's pretend you were at school
And you were ready to go home,
But you couldn't find your mitten.

You had the mitten
For your right hand,
But you couldn't find the one
For your left hand.

What would you do if
You couldn't find the mitten
For your left hand?

First you could look again
All by yourself.
Check in your coat pocket,
Look on the floor,
And search the top
Of your desk.

You could ask your friend
If he or she has seen
Your mitten.

If you still can't find
The mitten for your left hand,
Ask your teacher if she
Has seen your mitten.

Someone might have found it
And given your mitten
To your teacher.

If your teacher
Doesn't have it,
Someone might find it
And give your mitten
To your teacher
Tomorrow.

Teachers are good
At doing many things.
One good thing is
Giving back lost mittens
And hats and scarves
And nickels and pencils
And combs and barrettes
And almost everything.

If you find something
That isn't yours,
Take it to your teacher.

If you lose something,
And you look around for it
But can't find it,
Then go to the teacher
And ask her
To help.

Teachers are nice,
Kind people.

"Be kind to each other." (Eph. 4:32, TLB)

Playing Store

Another good thing about school
Is that you don't have to call
Your friends
And try to find someone
To play with.

When you get to school,
You will already have friends there,
And you can play together,
And you can work together.

Every day when you go to school,
You know there will be friends there,
And you will have someone
To play with.

Many children
Like to play store.
Maybe you will use blocks
For cans of food.
Maybe you will use paper
Instead of real money.

One person has to be
The storekeeper.
One, two or three people
Need to be the shoppers.

A shopper will come
To the store
And order a can of beans.
The storekeeper will

Give the shopper a block,
And the shopper will
Give the storekeeper
A piece of paper.

One time you can be
The storekeeper.
Another time you can be
The shopper.

It is fun to play
In school
Because you already have friends
At school.

What's a Crossing Guard?

There are many friendly people
Who work hard to help children
When they go to school.

One of the best helpers
Is the crossing guard.
A crossing guard stands
In the street and tells
Boys and girls
When to cross the street
And when to stand
On the sidewalk
And wait.

With many cars going past,
And many children walking
To school,
It's helpful to have someone
To tell children
When it is safe to cross.

A crossing guard might be
A man or a woman,
A boy or a girl.

A crossing guard usually
Wears something special.
It might be a special hat.
It might be a special coat.
It might be a special belt.

Sometimes a crossing guard
Carries a red stop sign.
The crossing guard
Will hold up the sign
To stop cars
Or to stop children.

When you go to school
For the first time,
Look for the crossing guard.

He is your friend.
If you do as he says,
Your walk to school
Should be extra safe.

My First Teacher

I can remember
My first teacher.
She was one
Of the nicest people
I had ever met.

My teacher was kind;
She was a good listener,
And she cared
About what happened
To me.

It made me feel good to know
That she would be at school
Each day
When I got there.

Today I know many teachers
Who like to be with children.
They have a good smile,
And they enjoy having children around.

They used to be little children, too.
One day they started school
Just the way you will.
Your teacher knows how you feel.
Your teacher went to school once,
Just the way you will.

Maybe you will see
Your teacher
At the grocery store,

Or working in her yard,
Or sitting in church,
Or at a picnic
In the park.

Look for your teacher.
She likes to do
The sames things
You like to do.

Send Your Parents Home!

School is so interesting
On the first day,
And there is so much to do
That some parents like
To stay around
After school starts.

It would be nice
If all the parents could stay,
But how would you get
Any schoolwork done
With thirty parents
Standing around?

The best thing to do is
Send your parents home
Right away!

The school you are going to
Is for children,
Not for adults.
You'd better
Send your parents home
Right away
So school can get started.

Tell your parents
That you will tell them
All about school
When school is over.

It would be best to
Send your parents home
Right away.

Parents have their job to do,
And you have your job to do
At school.
When you finish school
For that day,
You can tell them
All about it.

Story Time

Most of us like stories.
It's fun to have
Someone read to us
Even if we have heard the story
Over and over again.

Story time is part of the fun
Of going to school.

You will get to hear
Many amazing stories.

Maybe you will hear stories
About a friendly bear,
Or a tiger who is lazy,
Or an elephant who gets around
On roller skates.

Maybe you will hear stories
About children who live
In faraway places
And do things differently
Than you do them.

Maybe you will hear stories
About brave boys and girls
Who did daring
And interesting things.

Teachers are good storytellers.
They have done it often,
And they like to see children
Enjoying the story.

Sometimes the teacher
Will show pictures from the book
While she is reading.

Story time is part of what
Makes school so good.

It will be fun to see
What kinds of stories
Your teacher
Likes to read.

How Long Is School?

How many hours
Will you spend
In school
Each day?

Some kindergartens
Last for
Half a day.

You might go
To school
In the morning,
Or the afternoon.
You might not know
Which it will be
Until a few weeks before
School starts.

Many children
Go to school
For about
Three hours each day
When they first
Begin school.

In the first grade
The children will
Go to school
All day long.

At first
You will get tired
From doing so much.

Later, school will become
Easier and you might wish
You could stay longer.

Tying Your Shoes

Have you ever stepped
On your shoestring
And fallen down?

It can be dangerous
To walk or run
With your shoelace
Untied.

There will be so many
Good things to do
In school
That you won't want to
Keep stopping
To tie your shoe.

This would be
A good thing
To learn
Before you go
To school.

Every day you could practice
Tying your own shoes
In a tight, firm bow.

Then you will not have to
Stop so often
While you are
Enjoying school.

Working with Colors

Some of your time in school
Will be spent using colors.
Maybe you will draw with crayons,
Or with a paint brush,
Or paint with your fingers.

Painting with your fingers
Is especially fun.
You dip your fingers in
The slippery, wet paint
And make pictures on paper.

You might draw a house,
Or a dog, or a horse,
Or draw your brother or sister.

Sometimes the teacher will help
And make suggestions,
And your pictures will get
Better and better.

When you work with paint,
You will probably wear
An apron or an old shirt
To keep the paint
Off your clothes.

When you are finished,
You will wash your hands
And put things away
Very neatly.

Painting is fun
Because you can
Draw things
The way you
See them,
And use the colors
You like best.

God must like
To work with
Colors, too.

Maybe that's why
He made the grass
A bright green.

Maybe that's why
He made the sky
A light blue.

God must have
Enjoyed painting
The first rainbow.

**"I have placed my rainbow in the clouds."
(Gen. 9:13, TLB)**

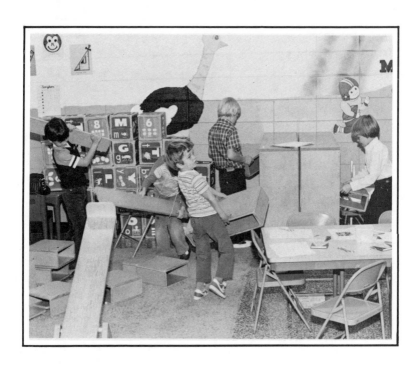

Help Your Teacher

Your teacher will be busy.
There is a lot to do
During a school day.

She will be busy
Answering your questions,
Putting pictures together,
Listening to your stories,
Reading stories,
Getting games ready,
And preparing music.

Your teacher
Won't be too busy
To help you, but
She will be busy.

That's why helpers
Are important
To your teacher.

She will need you
To pick up crayons,
To clean off your table,
To carry boxes,
To sit up straight
And be ready when
She wants to do
The next thing.

You will be a student
With a lot to learn.

You will also be a helper
Who does kind things
To help your teacher.

New Friends

You are meeting new friends
All of the time.

There might be children
Near your home.

Maybe you have relatives,
Like brothers or sisters,
Or maybe some cousins.

You probably have friends
At church or Sunday school.
As you grow older
You meet more people
And make more friends.

When you start school,
You will meet new people.
Maybe 10, 20, 30, or more.

Many of these new people
Will become your friends.

New friends are fun.
Some know games
You have never played before.
Some have funny stories
You have never heard before.

Some new friends
Will want to play
The kind of games
You like the best.

When you come home
You will be able
To tell your parents
The names of the new friends
You have met.

"Now you are my friends."
(John 15:15, TLB)

Learning Your Letters

You don't have to wait
Until you go to school
Before you start learning.

There are some things
You know already.

You learn some things
From television,
From Sunday school,
From playing school,
From your parents,

From hearing stories,
And many other ways.

Some children learn a lot
Before they go
To school.

Others have not learned
As much.

Either way is fine.

You will learn many new things
From your teacher.

Your teacher will help you learn
To read and print
Your letters—
Like A, B, C, D,
And many more.

Your teacher will help you learn
Your numbers, too—
Like 1, 2, 3, 4, 5, 6,
And many more.

It won't take long before
You know much more
Than you know now.

Learning letters and numbers
Can be a lot of fun,
And it will make you feel good
To see how much you can learn.

Some Safe Rules

When many children learn together,
Play together,
Run together,
And color together,
They need some rules
To be safe together.

Your teacher will explain the rules
So you will understand
And be able to obey them.

If you forget the rules,
Your teacher will explain them
Again.

There will probably be a rule
Against throwing things.
That rule will keep everyone
From getting hurt.

There will probably be a rule
Against running in the building.
That rule will keep you
From falling down.

There will probably be a rule
Against yelling in the school.
That rule will help you
To hear and learn better.

There will probably be a rule
Against pushing each other.

That rule will keep you
From getting hurt.

It's good to have rules
When people work and play
And learn and sing together.

Your teacher will carefully
Tell you the rules,
And if you forget the rules,
The teacher will explain them
Again.

Getting to School

There are so many ways
For children to get to school.

Many children walk to school
With their parents.
Others walk with a big brother
Or a big sister.

Some children walk with a neighbor,
And when they get older,
They walk to school by themselves.

I knew a lady who went to school
On a horse.
Some children still go to school
On horses!

Most children go to school
On a large school bus.
It stops near their homes
And brings them back again.

Some children live on islands,
And go to school on a boat.

Some children ride bikes
To school.

Often children get a ride to school
In their family car.

Learning to get to school
And back home again
Is part of growing up.

Little children can't
Go to school,
But you can, because
You are growing up.

How will you
Get to school
And home again?

Your parents will
Tell you how
To do it.
And they will help you.

Learning to Read

One of the best things
You will do in school
Is to learn to read.

Maybe you already know
A few words.
But you will learn
So many words
You can read an entire book
All by yourself.

You will be reading stories
About animals and circuses
And Indians and cowboys.

Someday you will be able
To read to little children,
And they will enjoy
Your interesting stories.

Your first year
Of school
Will open
A whole new world
Of learning.

"Teach a wise man, and he will be the wiser; teach a good man, and he will learn more." (Prov. 9:9, TLB)

The Playground

Have you ever been
To a real playground?

A school playground
Has special rides
For young school children.

Most children think
The playground
Is a special place
To play.

Your playground will have
An open area
Where you can run
Without going into
The street.

Maybe it will have
A set of swings
That are low enough
For you to sit on.

There might be a
Sliding board
That is silver-colored.

Many playgrounds
Have sets of shiny bars
To climb on.

Maybe your playground
Will have a ride

That many children sit on
While it turns
Around and around.

The playground is a special place
To run and play
And to laugh out loud.
Laughing is a good part
Of growing up
And learning.

"A time to laugh." (Eccles. 3:4, TLB)

Telling Time

When you go to school,
A clock will become
More important to you.

You will want to know
What time school starts.
You will want to know
What time school ends.

Your teacher
And your parents
Will carefully tell you
What time
Everything happens.

They will also remind you
Of the times
Until you remember them
By yourself.

Your schoolteacher
Will begin to teach you
How to tell time.

Once you learn
To tell time,
You will remember how
The rest of your life.

Some clocks have hands
That move around
And point to numbers.

Other clocks show
You the time
Without hands
But with lighted numbers.

You will enjoy learning
To tell time.

Being able to tell time
Is one more way
To know
You are growing up.

The Old and New

There will be many
Things in school
That will be new to you.

New people,
New words,
New toys,
New books,
New songs,
New games,
New stories,
And more.

There will also be
Some old things
That you have seen
Before.

When you get to school,
Look for things
You have seen before.

They won't all be there
But you will see
Many of them.

Tell your parents
If you see
A piano,
A television,
A record player,
A tape recorder.

You have seen
Some of these
Before.

Maybe you have seen them
At home,
At church,
At nursery school,
At a friend's house.

It will be exciting
To see new things.
It will be comforting
To see old things.

School is a wonderful place.

You Are
Growing Up

You probably can't remember,
But your parents used to
Do almost everything for you.

Every day your parents
Had to hold the spoon
And feed you.

They don't have to
Feed you now, because
You are growing up!

Every day your parents
Had to wash your hands
And your face.

They don't have to
Wash your hands
And face now, because
You are growing up!

Your parents used to
Put your clothes
On for you.

Your parents used to
Carry you around.

But now things
Are changing, because
You are growing up!

When you go to school
To work and play,
Everyone knows
You are growing up.

God has given you
A mind and a body
That you can use
At school.

It must make you
Feel good to know
You are growing up,
While God is
Watching over you.

"When her son was born they named him Samson, and the Lord blessed him as he grew up." (Judges 13:24, TLB)

Where Is Your School?

Do you know where
Your school building is?
Is it close to your house,
Or is it far away?

Have you ever driven
Or walked past
Your school?

Maybe you would like
Someone to take you
Past the school
Even if you have
Been there before.

It is good
To see the building
So you won't be
Surprised.

Maybe you would like
To go inside the building
With your parents.

You can see the halls
And the colorful classrooms
So it won't be
Strange to you.

Look for the playground.

What is there
That you will enjoy?

On the first day,
When you go to school,
You will already know
What the building
Looks like.

Then you won't be
Too surprised.

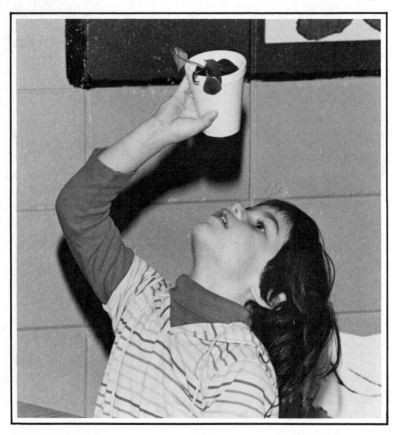

Plants Are for Growing

If you look carefully
Around your classroom,
You might find
Some plants growing
In flowerpots
Or in paper cups.

Plants often help us
Learn about the world
We live in.

We can look for
New leaves beginning to grow.
We can learn when
To add water
And when not to
Add water.

We can learn about
Tiny seeds that grow
Into big plants.

When we talk
About plants
We learn new words,
And we learn
To take turns talking,
And we learn
To take care of things.

Maybe your teacher
Will help start
A new plant.

And you can watch it
Come up through the earth
And spread its leaves,
And grow taller
And green.

You and your friends
And your teacher
Will learn as you watch
God's creation grow
All around you.

"Then God looked over all that he had made, and it was excellent in every way." (Gen. 1:31, TLB)

Obeying Your Teacher

School is going to be
Really good for you.
You will make
An excellent student.

One of the reasons
You will enjoy school
Is that
You have learned to obey.

That's important in school
With so many new things
To see and learn,
And with so many new students
Together for the first time.
Everyone needs to obey the teacher
So you can have a good class.

The teacher can tell which children
Are good at obeying.
They sit still when they are told
And stop talking when the class starts.
They keep their hands to themselves
All during the school day.

You help the teacher when you obey.
You help the other students.
You even help yourself
When you obey.

Sometimes a child will disobey
And break the rules of the class.
Then there is usually less time
To color, hear stories, play and learn.

If a child disobeys,
The teacher has to stop
And talk to him.
Then the whole class
Has to wait.

God wants children to obey
Parents and teachers.
You should be careful to obey
Because you want to be
A good student.

"Obey them that have the rule over you."
(Heb. 13:17, KJV)

Your Parents Went to School, Too

Years ago your parents
Did the same thing
You are about to do.

Your parents also went to school
For the first time.

It was a big day
In their lives.

It might be fun
To hear about
Their first day
At school.

Did they live
In a big city
Or a small town?

Did they go
To a large school
Or a small one?

Did their mother
Or father take them,
Or did they go with
A big brother or sister?

Can your parents

Still remember
Their first teacher?

What were some
Of the good things
Their first teacher did?

Did they take naps?
Did they have snacks?
Did they have blocks?
Did they have paints?
Did they write?
Did they sing?

It feels good
To talk to
Our parents.
They did many
Of the good things
You are going to do.

Enjoying Books

In a large, colorful classroom
There are many good books
With plenty of pictures.

Some of the books are for
The children to handle
And look through.

Many of these have colored pictures.
They are about bears and lions,
Long-necked giraffes and
Hairy baboons.

There are other books
Which your teacher uses.
Your teacher will read
These stories to you.

Maybe the teacher will
Read the story
More than once.
Children often like
To hear a story
More than once.

Books are special
And are to be treated
Carefully.

The pages are to be kept clean
And children should try hard
Not to tear them,
Or get clay on them,

Or spill orange juice
On them.

Books are like friends.
It feels good to have them
Around.

When they are treated
Carefully,
Books can stay around
A long time.

Seeing Pictures

How good are you
At seeing pictures
That aren't really there?

If someone said,
"Think about a brown dog
With a long tail
And a black nose
And floppy ears
And white paws,"
Could you picture that dog
In your mind?

There will be lots of times
When you will need
To see pictures in your mind.

Your teacher will tell
A story,
And as she tells it
You can picture
The dog or the bear
Or the car or the house
Or the girl or the boy
In your mind—
Just as if you were seeing
The picture.

That is part of what makes
Story time so good.
Children can see the story
Happening
As the teacher reads it.

Can you see a red fire truck?

Can you see a silver airplane?

Can you hear a train whistle?

Can you see a long-trunked elephant?

If you can see pictures
In your mind,
You must be ready
For school.

It's Time to Ask

When we talk about school,
There are many things we learn
That we didn't know before.

We find out about
Paint,
Snacks,
Playgrounds,
Blocks,
Teachers,
Coats,
Bathrooms,
And more.

But even if we talk about school
For many hours,
Sometimes we don't answer
That one question
You have been wondering
About.

No one knows
What that question is,
And they haven't answered
It yet.
But you know,
Because it's your question.

It's an important question
Because it is your question.

This would be a good time
To ask that question.

If your parent doesn't know
The answer,
He can find out
The answer.

If you have a question
About school,
Be sure to ask it.

Where Will Your Coat Go?

Have you ever thought about
What you will do with
Your coat or your sweater,
Or your hat
When you go to school?

You don't want to wear
Your coat all day long.
The room will be
Too warm for that.

And you don't want
To put your coat
On a table or a chair
And forget where
You left it.

That is why classrooms
Have special places
To hang your coats
Or sweaters or hats.

There might be a hook
To hang coats on.

There might be a place
With your name written
Over it.

Every day you can hang

Your coat there,
And every day
You can take it down
When it's time to go home.

Your teacher will tell you
What to do with your coat.

Teachers are good at
Helping children.

Meeting Your Teacher

Do you wonder
What your teacher will be like?
Your first teacher
Will probably be a woman,
But your teacher
Could be a man.

Your teacher will like children.
Your teacher will like *you*.
That is why she teaches
Kindergarten or first grade.

Your teacher wants
You to enjoy school,
Learn many things,
Play safely,
And be kind
To other children.

Your teacher is smart.
She went to college
To learn about children
And how to teach them.

She has a big smile
Which she uses most of the time.
She also has a frown
If someone doesn't obey.

Your teacher works hard

While you are in school.
She often works before school starts
And after school is over
To make your day interesting
So you will learn a lot.

She also keeps your classroom
Colorful and bright
With pictures and drawings
And a large, bright chalkboard.

Long ago, Jesus was also a teacher.
Sometimes He would teach adults,
And other times He taught
Young children
Just like you.

Jesus Christ was a good teacher.
Children enjoyed learning from Him.

"One day as the crowds were gathering, [Jesus] went up the hillside with his disciples and sat down and taught them there." (Matt. 5:1-2, TLB)

Eat a Good Breakfast

Each day before you
Go to school,
Try to eat a good breakfast.

Food makes you strong,
And strength is important
When you go to school
For two or three hours.

Some children don't like
To eat breakfast.

They want to eat just a little,
And later eat some candy
Or cookies.

A good meal is important
When you are growing up.
And if you are starting
To go to school,
You are growing up.

A good meal helps you
Think better.
A good meal helps you
Play better.
A good meal helps you
Work better.
A good meal helps you
Smile better.

Food is necessary
When you go to school.

**". . . And bread to give him strength."
(Ps. 104:15, TLB)**

Sharing

Do you have brothers and sisters?
Are there other children
Close to where you live?

When you play with them,
Do you share your toys
And books
And your bike?

It's good to share,
And most of the time
It's fun.

But once in a while
It's hard to share.
You don't want to let someone else
Play with something
That belongs to you.

Usually you are a good sharer.
That's going to help
When you go to school.

In your classroom
There will be 10, 20
Or even 30 children.

Sometimes you will need
To share crayons and paper
And toys and tables
And chalk, and much more.

Because you have already learned

To share, it will be easier for you.
When you share, the other children
Will want to share with you.

We all need
To learn
To give.

God gave His very best
When He sent
His only Son
Jesus Christ.

**"It is more blessed to give than to receive."
(Acts 20:35, TLB)**

Getting Tired

You know school can be fun,
Interesting and helpful.
Did you also know
School can make you tired?

When one of our children
First started school,
She would come home
Looking very tired.
Some days she would have to rest
Before she could do anything else.

Don't be surprised
If you become tired.
There is so much to do
And see and hear in school.
Some days you will want
To go home and lie down
And just rest.

That's all right.
Most children feel that way,
Especially during
The first few weeks of school.
Some schools even let you take
A short nap during the day.

When you get tired,
Try not to get grumpy,
Though that's easy to do.
The best thing is to rest,
Maybe eat a snack,

And soon you will
Feel better again.

"The Lord is my Shepherd; I shall not want. He maketh me to lie down in green pastures: he leadeth me beside the still waters." (Ps. 23:1, 2, KJV)

Traffic Lights

Are there any traffic lights
On your way to school?
You will learn to read them
If you don't know how already.

Some lights have words on them.
If the word "Walk" lights up,
You can walk across the street
After you look for cars
Coming around the corner.

If the word "Wait" lights up,
You should stay on the sidewalk
Until "Walk" appears again.

Maybe the words "Don't walk"
Will light up.
Then you stay on the sidewalk
Until you see "Walk."

If there are words
On the light,
Do not cross until
You see the word
"Walk."

Many streets have lights
Without words.
They have three lights:
Red, yellow, and green.

If the light is green,

You can cross the street.
If the light is red,
You cannot cross the street.
If the light is yellow,
It will soon turn red,
And you should stay
On the sidewalk
Until the green light
Comes on again.

If there is a traffic light
Near your house,
Your parents can
Show it to you
And explain what to do.

Traffic lights keep us safe
When we do what
They tell us to do.

"O Lord, you will keep me safe."
(Ps. 4:8, TLB)

Animals Go to School

Sometimes people
Bring animals to school
For children to see
And to pet.

But they don't bring animals
Unless they ask
The teacher first.

Maybe the teacher
Will bring an animal.

The animal might be
A brown rabbit,
Or a small hamster,
Or a kitten,
Or a puppy,
Or maybe a sheep.

When an animal comes,
The teacher talks
About the animal—
What it eats,
And where it lives.

Many times the children
Will get to touch it
Or pet it.

When children are as old
As you are,

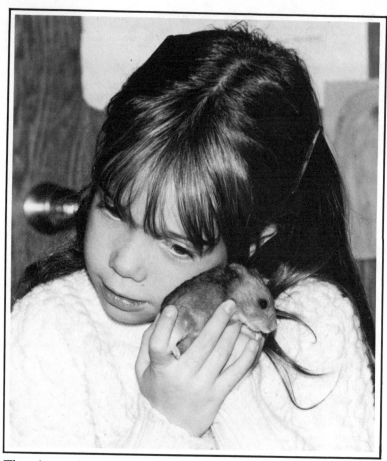

They know how to touch
Without hurting.

Talking about animals
Is part of learning
And going to school.

What kind of animal
Would you like to see
Come to school?

"Take a lesson from the ants."
(Prov. 6:6, TLB)

Learning Is Fun

School is an interesting place
Where you will learn
How to read books,
And write,
And put numbers
On paper.

Before long
You will know each letter—
A, B, C, D, E, F, and more.

Sometimes the teacher
Will read stories to you.
On other days you might
Listen to music.

It won't be all work.
You will get to play games.
But even while you are playing,
You will be learning something.

One day a boy brought
His baby puppies to class,
And everyone got to touch them.

Another day a girl brought
A large crab shell,
And everyone got to ask questions.

Learning can be fun
Because God made
Such an interesting world.

And when we learn
To read books,
And write,
And count better,
We will be able
To enjoy more of God's world
And the great things
He has made.

"A wise teacher makes learning a joy."
(Prov. 15:2, TLB)

It's Snack Time

Maybe your school will be
One that serves treats.
It will be okay if they
Don't serve a snack,
But it's extra nice
To get something to eat.

Your snack might be
A cup of cool, tasty
Orange juice.

Or else you could get
A carton of
Cold, fresh milk.

Along with your drink,
There might be a long
Graham cracker.

Or you could get
A round cookie
With chocolate chips,
Or creamy icing
On top.

In some schools
Each child brings
A cookie every day.

When it is near
Christmastime,
Easter,
Or Valentine's Day,

You might receive some
Special candy.

Maybe sometime
Another child
Will bring
A snack or some candy
To share with the class
On his birthday.

School is filled
With surprises
And good things
Like food.

**"Give us our food again today."
(Matt. 6:11, TLB)**

Going to Class

Have you ever been
In a classroom before?

Maybe you have gone
To Sunday school.
Going to school is like
Going to Sunday school,
Except
You go to school
Every day.

Maybe you have gone
To nursery school.
Going to school is like
Going to nursery school,
Except
The children are older,
Like you are now.

Maybe you have watched
Children in a classroom
On television.
Going to school is like
Watching school on television,
Except
You are really there.

A school classroom
Will be new
And exciting
Because you will learn
Many wonderful things.

Do You Enjoy Music?

We have music all around us.
We hear it on television,
On radios and record players.
We hear music on tape recorders.
And some of us have pianos,
Trumpets, guitars or other instruments
In our homes.

You probably have a few songs
You like best.
You have listened to them
Over and over again.

If you like music,
You will enjoy it at school.
Many classes teach children
By using music.

Some classrooms have
Record players and tape recorders.
Many have easy instruments
For children to play.
A few classrooms
Even have pianos.

On some days
You may get to sing
Or march.

You will even learn stories
By singing about them.
Don't be surprised if one day
You bring a new song home
And sing it to your parents.

God made people
In a special way
So we could enjoy music.

Teachers use music
In a special way
To help us learn.

"Forever and ever I will sing about the tender kindness of the Lord!"
(Ps. 89:1, TLB)

Taking Turns

When you are in a group
And you want to say something,
How are you going to be heard
With so many people around?

There can't be ten people
All talking at one time.
If they did, you couldn't
Be heard.

That's why it is important
To learn how to take turns.

When someone else is talking,
You will listen, quietly.
When you are talking,
The others will listen, quietly.

Many teachers ask the children
To raise their hands
If they want to talk.
Then the teacher will call on them
And listen to what
They have to say.

That is a good way
To learn to take turns.
Maybe your teacher
Will have another way.

When we take turns,
All of us get to share

And ask questions
And tell important things
That happened to us
Or that we saw.

Taking turns
Is one of the best things
About going to school.

**"A time to be quiet; a time to speak up."
(Eccles. 3:7, TLB)**

The Bulletin Board

Do you have a special place
In your home
To pin up notes
Or pictures or letters?

These are called cork boards,
Or message boards,
Or bulletin boards.

Schools have large,
Long, bulletin boards.

They are neat to have
Because so many
Interesting things
Are put on them.

Your teacher might
Put pictures on them,
Or cut out paper leaves
And pin them on a paper tree.

In the winter
You might find
Pictures of snowy hills
Or a round snowman
On the bulletin board.

In the spring
You might find
Pictures of green leaves
And red-breasted robins.

Sometimes the teacher
Will put children's papers
On the bulletin board.

Maybe someday
Your painting,
Or your printing,
Or your paper leaves
Will be put up on
The bulletin board.

Bulletin boards are
Special places in
School classrooms.

It's Nice to Know

It's nice to know
How to print your name,
But what if you don't
Know how?

It's nice to know
How to write numbers,
But what if you don't
Know how?

It's nice to know
How to paint,
But what if you don't
Know how?

Everything will be okay
If you can't print,
If you can't count,
If you can't paint.

Because,
You will learn all of these
While you're in school.

That's why you have a teacher,
So you can learn the things
You do not know.

Your teacher understands children.
Your teacher likes children.
Your teacher enjoys children.
Your teacher will help you
Learn the things
You do not know.

Other Books in this Series by the Same Author